JAN BRETT

Comet's Nine Lives

SCHOLASTIC INC.

New York Toronto London Auckland Sydney

For Sean and Yun

ISBN 0-590-10972-3

Copyright © 1996 by Jan Brett.
All rights reserved. Published by Scholastic Inc., 555 Broadway, New York, NY 10012, by arrangement with G. P. Putnam's Sons, a division of The Putnam & Grosset Group.

SCHOLASTIC and associated logos are trademarks and/or registered trademarks of Scholastic Inc.

21 20 19   3 4 5 6/0

Printed in the U.S.A.   40
First Scholastic printing, September 1997

Comet was born thirty miles out to sea on Nantucket Island. He grew up wandering all over the island, staying a few days here and a few days there.

One summer day Comet stopped in a garden to nibble some tasty looking foxgloves. First they made him feel woozy. Then he fell into a deep sleep.

When Comet woke up, he felt fine, but
different. *Oops!* He realized he'd lost the first
of the nine lives every cat has when it is born.

Maybe I should find myself a home.
And he trotted into the bookstore and settled
down on top of a stack of bestsellers.

Life was good until one day it rained all morning and
the islanders hurried inside for something to read.
In the rush, Comet's tower of bestsellers toppled over
and he was buried under a pile of books. *Oh, no!*
He had turned the page on life number two.

I think I need some fresh salt air.
Down to the docks he went and arrived just as a
little scalloper, the *Jean T*, was casting off. Once
under way, an easterly wind blew up and Comet
knew he had made a mistake.

Up, up the *Jean T* rose. Down, down, down she flew on a following sea. Comet hung on until a huge wave foamed across the stern and he found himself afloat on the high seas.

The tide carried Comet back into the harbor, but
as he flicked the salt from his whiskers, life number
three went out with the tide.

Comet was still recovering on the beach when he heard music. It was the annual Fourth of July concert. He climbed up a tree for a better look.

Four

The music reached its loudest chord. Comet got so excited that he lost his grip and plunged down into the tuba. Three waltzes and a Sousa march later, Comet staggered away, and life number four sounded its last chord.

Maybe I'm trying too hard. It's time for some fun!
He climbed into a bike basket just as a crowd of
summer visitors were hurrying off the ferry.

It was Waffles' first time on the island.
She was happy to have Comet's company,
and off they went bumpity, bump all around
the island. Just as they reached the bottom
of the last hill into the village, Waffles
screeched to a halt to avoid a taxi.

Six

Comet went flying, along with life number six.
I think I'll just walk the rest of the way.

Comet was limping by the island theater when a poster
advertising the last performance of summer caught his eye.
A beautiful actress with a sweet smile looked out at him.
Maybe she would like to take a cat home with her.

Comet pranced happily on stage and purred loudly. The actress sneezed. "There's a cat in here!" she shrieked. "I'm allergic to cats!" She spotted Comet and hurled her sequined high heel right at him.

Comet flew through the air into the last row. The
curtain had come down on life number seven!

Fall breezes were blowing up as the summer visitors
headed for the ferry. Comet wandered alone along the
beach. He could see the red beacon of the Brant Point
lighthouse in the distance.

Waves crashed and pounded on the sand. The wind picked up and deck chairs and lobster pots flew by Comet. It was Hurricane Elmadore heading straight for Nantucket Island. All Comet could see now was the blinking lighthouse beacon. He ran toward it when a huge wave broke on top of him.

Eight

The rushing surf carried Comet into an open doorway, as life number eight washed out to sea. Dazed, he opened his eyes and saw a green light across the room.

"Meow," someone purred.

"Meow," he answered, looking up.

He was staring into the green eyes of the lighthouse cat. At that moment, he knew he was home.

And as the fall days turned into winter, Comet knew
exactly where he wanted to live for the rest of his life.